Kidnapped!

Introduction — Volume 5: The End of the Quest

In June 1751, upon his parents' death, 16-year-old **David Balfour** left the small Scotland town of Essendean to travel to "the house of Shaws," the estate of his only living relative, **Ebenezer Balfour**. The uncle proved a greedy old man, living in a huge, decaying old house, who tried to trick David into falling to his doom from a great height. David came to believe that his late father **Alexander** was the older brother and should have inherited the estate.

Ebenezer lured David to the Queensferry docks on the promise he could speak with a lawyer named **Rankeillor**, who knew the Balfour family's history. But Ebenezer had secretly arranged for David to be kidnapped to sea by a **Captain Hoseason** of the Covenant. At sea, the ship struck a small boat, whose only survivor was **Alan Breck Stewart**. Alan was an exiled Scottish Jacobite—one who desired to see the British throne go to James of Scotland, whose supporters had been brutally defeated half a decade earlier. When Captain and crew tried to seize Alan's belt-full of gold, the Scot and David teamed up to seize the ship's main cabin. Soon afterward, however, David fell overboard amid surging breakers, while the ship was borne away.

Reaching civilization, David learned Alan had survived the Covenant's sinking. Following instructions to join the rebel in Scotland, David encountered **Colin Campbell (The Red Fox)**, a despised nobleman who planned to expel Scottish tenants from their lands. Campbell was shot and killed—and David suspected Alan of the deed, though he denied it. The pair fled across the Highlands. When David became ill from exposure, they sought shelter at the cottage of **Duncan Dhu** of the Maclarens. One night, **Robin Oig**, son of the notorious Campbell outlaw chief Rob Roy, came to the house—and he and Alan at once renewed an old quarrel. Insulting each other, they were on the verge of drawing their swords….

Writer: Roy Thomas

Penciler: Mario Gully

Inker: Jason Martin

Colorist: Sotocolor's

A. Crossley

Letterer: David Sharpe

Cover Artist: Dennis Calero

Production: Tom Van Cise

Special Thanks –

Sankovitch, Allo, Ginter, Nausedas

Associate Editor: Nathan Cosby

Senior Editor: Ralph Macchio

Editor in Chief: Joe Quesada

Publisher: Dan Buckley

Spotlight

VISIT US AT
www.abdopublishing.com

Reinforced library bound edition published in 2011 by Spotlight, a division of the ABDO Group, 8000 West 78th Street, Edina, Minnesota 55439. Spotlight produces high-quality reinforced library bound editions for schools and libraries. Published by agreement with Marvel Characters, Inc.

Printed in the United States of America, Melrose Park, Illinois.
042010
092010
♻ This book contains at least 10% recycled material.

Library of Congress Cataloging-in-Publication Data

Thomas, Roy, 1940-
  Kidnapped! / adapted from the novel by Robert Louis Stevenson ; adapted by: Roy Thomas ; illustrated by: Mario Gully. -- Reinforced library bound ed.
     p. cm.
  "Marvel."
  Summary: Retells, in comic book format, Robert Louis Stevenson's tale of sixteen-year-old David Balfour who, after being kidnapped by his villainous uncle, escapes and becomes involved in the struggle of the Scottish highlanders against English rule.
  ISBN 978-1-59961-781-7 (vol. 1) -- ISBN 978-1-59961-782-4 (vol. 2) -- ISBN 978-1-59961-783-1 (vol. 3) -- ISBN 978-1-59961-784-8 (vol. 4) -- ISBN 978-1-59961-785-5 (vol. 5)
  1. Scotland--History--18th century--Juvenile fiction. 2. Graphic novels. [1. Graphic novels. 2. Scotland--History--18th century--Fiction. 3. Adventure and adventurers--Fiction.] I. Gully, Mario. II. Stevenson, Robert Louis, 1850-1894. Kidnapped. III. Title.
  PZ7.7.T518Kid 2010
  741.5'973--dc22
                                    2009052844

All Spotlight books have reinforced library bindings and are manufactured in the United States of America.

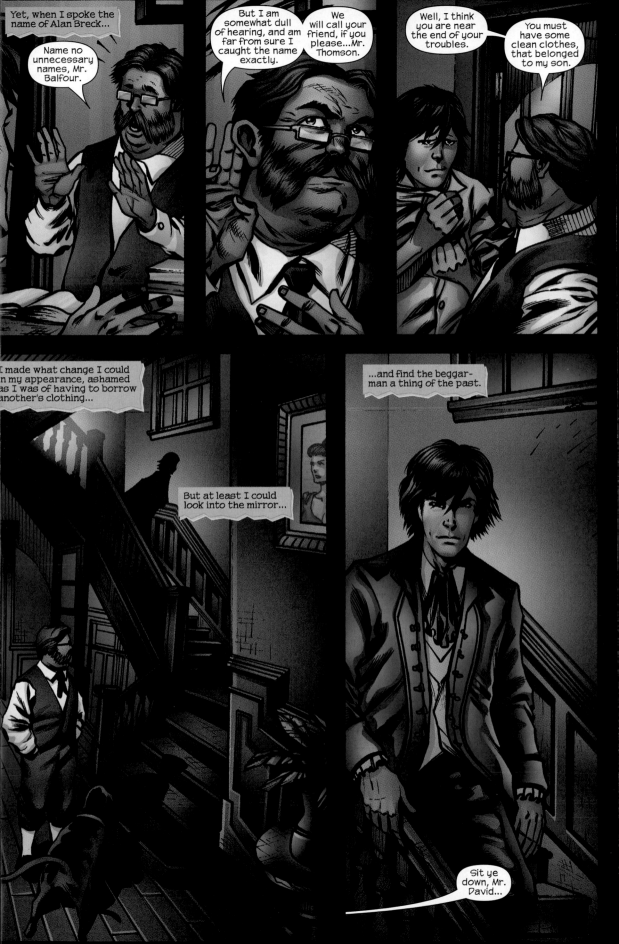

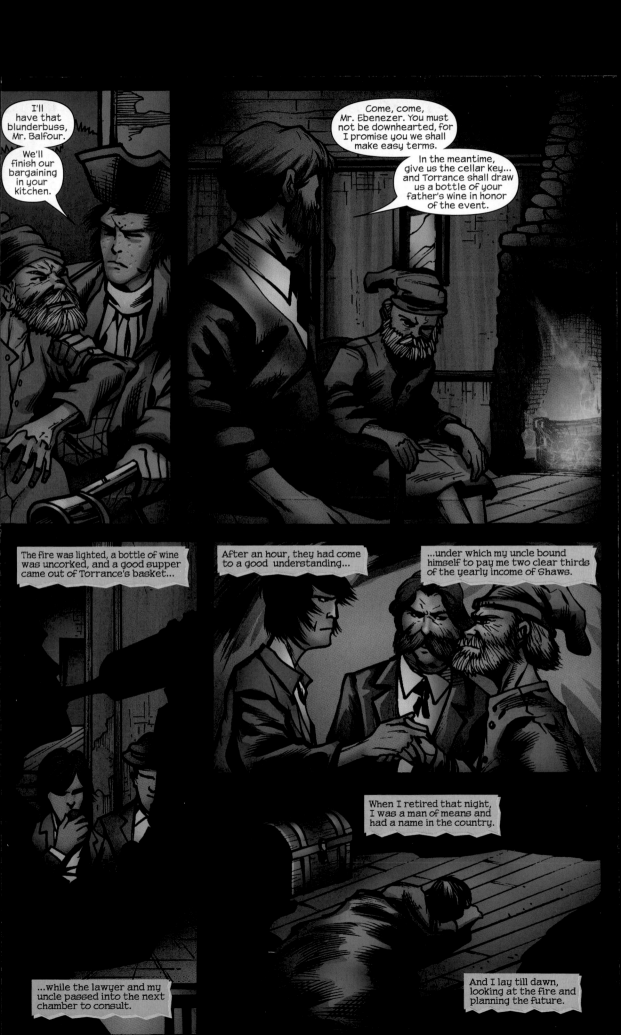

Fin--